S
.2

Willard, Nancy
    The lively anatomy of God.   Eakins
Pr. [1968]
    95 p.

4.95

THE LIVELY ANATOMY OF GOD

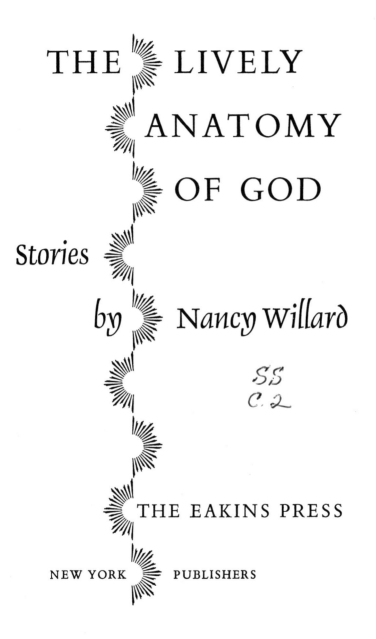

THE LIVELY ANATOMY OF GOD

Stories

by Nancy Willard

THE EAKINS PRESS

NEW YORK PUBLISHERS

A celebration: for Denise, Konstantinos, and Eric

Contents

"For this is the most hidden of my commandments:
Ye shall play before My countenance."

ILSE AICHINGER *Die grössere Hoffnung*

THE

HUCKLEBONE

OF A SAINT

The Hucklebone of a Saint

I N MY father's house, moral ambiguity was not allowed. It was considered unhealthy, like soft drinks and candy, not to be kept in the house and to be eaten only with reprimands that kept you from enjoying it. As a result of this stricture, until I was ten my father and I saw little of each other. We had a nodding acquaintance at meals, during which he listened to the news on the radio and spoke to no one. When I heard his car crunching up the driveway at night, bringing him back from the laboratory where he worked both morning and evening, I knew I should be asleep.

It was my mother who gave me my faith in the black arts which came to dire fruition in my tenth year. Faith takes root in the insignificant. We would be sitting around the dinner table and I would drop my knife.

"Pick it up Anne-Marie," my father would say. Or perhaps he would say nothing, but I would feel a discomforting frown.

"A man is coming," my mother would add.

Or if I dropped a spoon:

"A child is coming."

I never thought to notice whether or not the prophecies came true. I only remembered that if you dropped a knife, a man would visit the house for certain. Not that day, perhaps, nor the next, but some time when you did not expect it. When you had even forgotten you dropped the knife.

My father did not recognize the power of a knife to bring a visitor any more than he recognized the power of an umbrella opened indoors to bring bad luck. Knowing that differences exist most peacefully under one roof when they are unaware of each other, my mother did not practice her black arts openly before him. If she knocked over the saltcellar while clearing the table, she brushed a small pile of salt aside and waited till he was napping before she threw a pinch of it into the fire. She knew he would ask, just as I asked, and he would be harder to answer:

"Why?"

"Judas spilled salt at the Last Supper. And look what happened to him."

I had seen da Vinci's "Last Supper" hanging like an enormous postcard in the Sunday School parlor of the Lutheran Church, and I resolved to look for the salt.

"See for yourself. It's lying on the table by Judas' hand, just like it's lying on our table now."

"But just because Judas had bad luck, why should I have it?"

"Just because."

Not because one man, this particular man had had it, certainly. The more I thought about it, the more I knew I could not inherit Judas' bad luck the way you inherit the color of your eyes and the shape of your face. Rather, in spilling the salt he had somehow stumbled upon a law. Others had probably discovered it before him. But it took the Crucifixion and Potter's Field before its validity was recognized.

It occurred to me that there must be many such laws I did not know. It had never worried me before. I knew it was my father's business to find out the laws which kept the world running. When he took me to the laboratory with him, I saw that it was full of things whose secrets he was wresting.

"What are those pretty stones?"

"Those are minerals."

"Why do you keep them in that funny box?"

"Because they're radioactive."

It was his pleasure to open the laws that lay hidden in things and make them clear, so clear that I could touch them with my hands whenever I picked up the models of molecular structures he kept in a little glass case on his desk. What he found was beautiful and utterly irrelevant to the way I lived my life. The world would go on turning whether my father or anyone else's father found out why. To discover the law of gravity, for example, was only to name what you already knew. It didn't change a thing.

The uselessness of my father's laws made them easier to learn than my mother's. He had marvellous instruments to extend the range of the senses and reach into the very cells of being. And when you found one law, you found others contingent on it. Whereas the laws in my mother's world were utterly capricious. You stepped on a crack and if your mother's back broke, you knew you'd found the reason. There were no conclusions, only an infinite number of particular cases.

And knowing the laws that worked in particular cases did not free you from the fear of breaking them. It only committed you more deeply to a power that gave you nothing in return for your obedience except the vague feeling that you were somehow maintaining the status quo.

As soon as I acknowledged the existence of my mother's laws, life became immensely more complicated. Since each law was a particular event, the smallest events suggested themselves as a possible means of discovery. Riding my bicycle, for example, I would innocently imagine that if the stoplight turned red before I reached it, something bad would happen. If it didn't, things would stay the same. Nothing good would happen, but nothing bad would, either. Once I had decided it might be so, the game became real. The stoplight had the power to direct the traffic of my future. I began to avoid stoplights.

Other events acquired a similar authority which had to be countered with rituals and taboos. Certain dresses brought bad luck and hung unworn in the closet. Tuesdays meant low marks on spelling quizzes and mistakes in mathematics.

The most discouraging part of the whole business was that it was so much easier to bring bad luck on oneself than good luck. It was so much easier to break a mirror and live in the shadow of impending misfortune than to count a hundred white horses and wish for happiness.

As the games I invented mysteriously turned into statutes, I believed that I was maintaining the even keel of our joys until one day I came home from school to find two suitcases in the front hall. Grandmother was coming to live with us.

She was to live out her life in our guest room, which quickly took on the color and smell of her life. It was a cold room, shut off from the house, with a pink satin bolster on the bed and doilies on the dressing table and a clean blotter on the desk; one of those anonymous rooms often slept in and rarely lived in, like a room in a hotel. Now the bolster gave way to a dozen eiderdowns. The radiators clanked and pounded; the room was kept at eighty. My grandmother went about in heavy underclothes and sweaters and seldom left her quarters for more tepid parts of the house.

Further, its innocent spaces were suddenly thronged with medicine bottles of all kinds: lecithin, calcium, supplementary organic pills, keopectic, and Hexylresorcinol. There were also cases of vitamins, each regulating some function of the body and therefore necessary, Grandmother believed, to its survival. She kept a reserve supply of everything in her suitcase which I observed was never wholly unpacked.

On the wall over her bed hung a Chinese painting of a mountain. This she disliked, though she never asked us to take it down.

"Mountains! What good are mountains? You can't farm land like that."

Her chief amusement was going to church. She listened to the sermon with great attentiveness but could never remember a word of it afterwards. She enjoyed the music and the feeling of being united with so many people for the good of their souls, which she had been taught was the only good. Its attainment was always linked in her mind with programs of self-improvement and the systematic acquisition of virtues, which she wrote down on little snatches of paper, found in odd corners of the room long after she ceased to live there.

She passed her days with what I considered an unbearable monotony. In the morning my mother brought up her oatmeal and orange juice on a tray. Grandmother sat at the dressing table and ate in front of the mirror while my mother combed her long white hair into two braids and pinned them crosswise on her head. Then my mother went down to the cellar to hang up the wash—for it was early April when my grandmother came, and too cold to hang clothes outside—always listening for the sound of the old woman's voice.

"Daughter?"

"I'm right here."

Assured she was not alone, Grandmother would set about arranging the accoutrements of her life, that is, the contents of the suitcase. In addition to her impressive collection of medicines, she kept extra sets of heavy underwear and rolls of toilet paper which she sometimes unwound and wadded into her garters like an amulet to ward off attacks of nervous diarrhea.

It seemed to me that she was pursuing a secret journey, the destination of which constantly evaded her. Sometimes she would come to lunch wearing her hat and her big sealskin coat, inquiring about bus schedules, hinting that she had not been well-treated. My mother's response was always the same.

"There are no buses today. It's a holiday."

"Ah, then, I'll have to wait."

Then she would mention her responsibilities at the house in Coronna which she had so recently left and where my mother had grown up. Men were coming to pick the cherries in the orchard; she had to look sharp that they did not cheat on the hours. Grandfather, long gone, was waiting for her; who would fix his dinner? She would explain it to us with pathetic urgency.

My mother maintained the illusion through a round of outings which never got the woman to her destination but only postponed the total collapse of her reason.

Grandmother's favorite escort on these outings was her brother Oskar. He was seventy-one, seven years younger than my grandmother. To me he was ageless, a spry, dapper little man who always wore two-toned Oxfords and a black and yellow vest giving him the look of a frail and friendly bee. He was retired, not from any single occupation, but from a great variety of them, including brief stints as homesteader, circus barker, undertaker's assistant and shortstop for an obscure ball team in Minnesota. He had once had a wife and child, both of whom were dead, and I remember neither.

Sometimes he wrote poems—jingles, he called them—on the placemats he got every noon at Howard Johnson's, surfaces as suggestive to him as marble to Michelangelo, their floral borders and bright colors concealing clusters of language. Slipping a finely folded jingle into my hand, he would greet me with a mock bow, his shoes twinkling.

"Ah, Miss Callard," he would say.

"Oh, Bowser, how I've missed you."

That was in honor of the candies he kept in his pockets, Callard and Bowser's Plain Jane Toffees, or Lady Fingers, or Licorice. If he had no candy, then I knew he was bringing a game, a cardtrick, perhaps, or a Cracker Jack toy. My mother justified his passion for Cracker Jack by saying it reminded him of baseball, but I could see well enough how he broke into smiles of satisfaction when the toy appeared at the bottom of the box. Of all his presents he said, with a mixture of shame and pride,

"It's nothing; I got it for pennies."

He would drive Grandmother around town to parade, as he called it, in my father's car. Sometimes I went along, sitting alone in the back seat.

"You want to take the wheel, my girl?" he suggested, turning solemnly to his sister.

Grandmother looked at him with horror.

"You used to do very well. I remember how we had the only car in Deep River, and how you used to make me get out at every corner and look in all directions to see if another one was coming."

Her early scruples eventually overcame her, for when my mother was fourteen, Grandmother drove the car into the garage and forgot to take it out again. No one else in the family had a license, so there it remained while my grandmother thought of more and more reasons for walking to this place and that, until it was understood that the car was now part of the house, as immovable as the walls and the floor.

On Sundays my uncle came for breakfast, bringing with him a small flute of his own carving. He never went with us to church but waited at the house to join us for dinner, after which he retired to the sun room for a nap. He slept with his eyes open for about an hour and then I would hear him talking to the flute, as if he had no idea of gaining my audience.

"There was an organ in the house where we grew up. All the German farm houses had them. Your grandmother used to sit in the parlor and play it by the hour."

"Where is it now?" I had always wanted to play an organ but thought that all organs were indissolubly joined to churches.

Oskar shook his head.

"The spitzwinks took it."

It was the German farmers in Iowa who told Oskar about the spitzwinks. Sometimes the crops failed because of rain, sometimes because of drought. And sometimes they failed for no reason at all. Then the farmers said, "Ah, the spitzwinks have done it." The spitzwinks made holes in your best stockings and chipped the cups and saucers that you used every day. They were the reason that plants marked "annuals" on the box at the market would not return in the spring.

"But why didn't Grandpa Wiedow lock up the organ so the spitzwinks wouldn't steal it? Didn't he know there'd be other children?"

"He never thought of it."

The spitzwinks, I thought, were a sort of game, with no more substance than a figure of speech. But as weeks turned into months and Grandmother stayed on, I soon saw them as a name for forces which enmeshed her in propitiatory rituals far more suffocating than my own.

When she was dressed for bed and had drunk the hot milk that my mother brought her, she closed her door and began the long process of barricading it. Lying in my bed I could hear the moving of furniture, the heaviest pieces in the house and a chilling testimony of my grandmother's strength. A long slow scraping across the floor was the chest of drawers. Then came the slow bump of the dressing table with the oval mirror that did not move so easily because the castors had disappeared. And finally I heard a persistent scuffling sound, as if my grandmother were waging a battle with the forces of darkness. In half an hour the sounds ceased but the light still shone under her door; she was awake.

"Margaret, did you lock the front door?"

That was my mother, who always sounded like somebody else when anyone called her by her first name.

"Yes!" My father was already asleep; he left to my mother the responsibility of answering.

For a few minutes it would be still. Then you heard the furniture moving again, the chest of drawers, the dressing table, the chair. This time, it was being forced away from the door. When the door opened, Grandmother's voice sounded near. She had stepped into the hall.

"I say, did you lock the front door?"

"Yes, of course!"

"I think I'll just go down and try it."

Like the soul of an extinct bird she glided swiftly down the stairs, her two braids springing out over her ears just as they fell when she took out the pins. She rattled the knob of the front door for us all to hear.

"Good. I just wanted to be sure."

Then her own door would slam, as if she had reached her room in a single bound. And presently the moving of furniture would begin again.

Night after night I acknowledged the danger that lay in such defences. Clearly my grandmother's rituals only brought her closer to the fears she wished to avoid. Mine were still part of the games that a child plays when by an act of the imagination he wills his own life into what has none for the sake of companionship. If my grandmother's rituals were a game, then it must be a game that she played with deadly earnest, the stakes to be paid with her own life. Whenever I recognized this, I had the uncomfortable feeling that we were becoming more and more alike.

What linked us was a discovery that the faith we had gathered from generations of Sundays was no match for this greater faith in the reality of darkness. Where did it come from? We had not invited it. Who put it into my heart that the darkness under the bed gathered itself into invisible hands, waiting to snatch my feet when I groped my way back from the bathroom at night? How was it that my mother, my father, and Uncle Oskar stepped quietly into their beds with no knowledge of this danger and therefore no fear? How could you lose your freedom without knowing who had taken it? If my faith in the darkness could not be broken, then it was not faith as I knew it but a love for all that could not be named and a secret desire that it never should be.

Because of this love my mother wore her best dress wrong side out to my cousin's wedding for fear of bringing bad luck on the heads of the newly wedded pair. Because of this love she knocked on wood whenever she spoke of my achievements in school and asserted half-jokingly—but only half—that Thomas Dewey had lost the presidential election

20

because he had a horseshoe hanging upside down over his door and all his luck drained out. She had grown up in a neighboring town and seen for herself the quiet gnawing emblem of his doom which, if heeded, might have changed the course of nations.

By day Grandmother's diversions alternated between drives, church, and Abby's beauty parlor. The beauty parlor and the church stood kitty corner from each other on a block named by persecuted German immigrants who wanted their children to grow up on Liberty Street. The slow but ceaseless arrival of new settlers gave it such a vivid restlessness that even now I think of it not as a place but as a way of being alive.

The excitement began early in the morning when men in white overalls streaked with blood hauled carcasses from trucks to the back of the butcher shop. But when its doors opened for business, the very memory of blood had been quenched. Sausages were hung high on the ceiling, tucked out of sight like poor relations, to be asked for by name but not displayed. On shelves that ran the length of the shop you found cocoa from Holland in delftware jars, flatbread from Norway and flowered tins of gumdrops from Paris.

Abby had her beauty shop above the butcher's, and it was there that I met Mary Ellen. She was two years older than I and had the job of answering the telephone and unwrapping the little pieces of cotton which Abby tucked into the hairnets of her customers to protect their ears from the sirocco blasts of the dryer. She also kept the glass atomizers filled with the heavy scented lacquer which "set" the finger waves so that hair came out dry and rippling as dunes of sand.

In exchange for these favors Abby allowed her to read the movie magazines she kept by the dryers. Mary Ellen devoured the legends of her favorites as faithfully as she attended Mass. The stars were her secular saints, their changeless identities to be consulted in the minute crises of daily life. She borrowed a gesture from one, a hair style from another, all, I thought, to no effect. There was a faint aura of dirt about everything she wore, like a shading sketched on the original color, and as she washed the pins and curlers, customers would stare at her fingernails in amazement. For she did not believe in cleaning them; she simply bit the dirty portion away, peeling it with great fastidiousness like a delicate fruit.

In warm weather we walked to the vacant lot behind a funeral parlor where we could play undisturbed. The only other building on it was a warehouse full of coffins. Squeezing among them like bankers checking their safes, we would collect the number of different kinds, the way you collect out-of-state license plates or the number of white horses you pass when you are traveling. Most of the coffins were dark and plain. We decided it was lucky to find a baby's coffin because we found them so seldom. A few of the large ones were scrolled, and we watched for these too, though their luck was considered less potent. At the end of the day we remembered how many we had found.

Or rather I remembered how many we had found. I had come to believe that the luck things carried augmented like interest only if I kept my books straight, never forgetting how much I had saved. When the total number of white horses, license plates, loads of hay, baby coffins, and other spectacles deemed lucky by us grew too large to keep in my head, I wrote the sums down in a little notebook with the conviction that it was both useless and necessary to some final reckoning of my fate.

By this time the last platoon of Abby's customers would

be touching their brittle curls as they emerged from under the dryers. Grandmother never sat under the dryer as it threw her into a panic and she would roll her eyes about like a horse being pushed into a van. With her hair pinned in wet braids across her head, she turned the pages of the movie magazines, clucking at the wages of sin, until my mother emerged with her hair pitilessly knotted into ringlets.

"It's so hard to find someone who can do my hair plain the way I like it," she would say.

Abby's hair-dos were utterly without style. She believed in durability rather than immediate effect. She made pincurls so tight that they kept their kink for days and only ceased to remind you of sheep's wool or fiji chieftains a week later. On her walls hung photographs showing a wide variety of styles but no matter which one you ordered you always came out looking the same. This attracted a host of elderly ladies whose conservative taste could not be met in the salons uptown where ratting and backcombing were the fashion.

Although I knew Abby had been a widow oftener than some wives have been mothers, I could not imagine her in love. She was a stocky figure in her white smock with sparse brown hair and thick glasses, and as she tipped your head into the sink and scrubbed your scalp she sang at the top of her voice:

> *When you're smiling,*
> *When you're smiling,*
> *The whole world smiles with you.*

And while she sang, always a little breathless from reaching and scrubbing, she talked and talked and her bosom heaved like a full sail over your face. Neither I nor my mother knew any of the people she talked about except as we might feel we knew the characters in a radio serial—Pearl, Maria, Charley, and all the others whose foibles she expounded to us according to her mood.

"He's gone to see that widow lady downstairs, that's what. He lies around on her bed all day and she feeds him white albacore tuna. It's nothing but grub what he's after, a heartless beast, no feelings at all."

Not for a long time did I learn that many of the names I associated with people actually belonged to cats. Abby fed all the stray cats that came to her door and demanded in exchange a scrupulous fidelity. If one stayed away for two days or a week, she railed against him like a forsaken lover.

With Grandmother, however, she never spoke of cats. Every conversation was an exchange of ailments and remedies, Grandmother defending her drugstore prescriptions and Abby speaking for her teas. Among her rinses she kept a packet of alba camomile, the label of which showed a man coming out of a forest and handing a spray of blossoms to a little girl. To me that alone argued for its magical properties.

"Someday you'll be drinking a good dose of henna if you're not careful, keeping it all mixed up like that," warned my mother.

But Abby's cupboard contained a greater wonder than alba camomile tea. It was locked away in a small chest behind the bleaches and dyes. Sometimes when all her customers were safely tucked under the dryers and time lay heavy on her hands, she would bring it out for Mary Ellen and me to look at.

"It's the hucklebone of a saint," explained Abby.

I did not dare to ask what a hucklebone was and decided that it was the place on your elbow that tingled when you accidentally bumped it against a table or chair. I have since learned that it is the anklebone.

24

The tiny splinter of bone lay pressed between two discs of glass in the middle of a brass sun from which crude rays emanated. Abby's grandfather, a connoisseur of the marvellous, had bought it in the catacombs outside Rome from a priest who took him through by the light of a serpent twisted around his staff. At Cologne he had kissed the skulls of the Magi and the nail driven into Christ's right foot; at Trèves he had touched part of the thigh of the Virgin Agatha and seen the devil carrying the soul of his grandmother in a wheelbarrow. He had walked on the holy stair of St. John Lateran and wagered for a tooth of St. Peter. He lost the wager but the same day he was miraculously healed of a lifetime of headaches by combing his hair with the comb of a saint.

"Which saint?" asked Mary Ellen.

"I don't know. What does it matter?"

I liked the saints, faded as they were in the liturgies of my church. I liked them because they attended so patiently to the smallest human catastrophes. If you lost something you went to St. Anthony. If you wanted a husband you went to St. Nicholas. Even thieves found a comforter among the ranks of the blessed who would not turn a deaf ear to their problems.

I had need for such a comforter. Since my grandmother's arrival my dependence on the dark powers had grown steadily worse. I had come to believe that certain words released the forces of evil, being part of that vast body of laws of which spilling salt was only a tiny amendment. All my life words had come to me wrapped in feelings that had nothing to do with their meanings and everything to do with the way my hand felt when I printed them. But now they lost all connection with the things they named and took on the opacity of a magic formula. Not being able to say *tree* didn't mean that trees were evil. It only meant that saying the name released forces beyond your control.

Perfect obedience led, clearly, to perfect silence, and the slow death of all my delights. You cannot serve two masters. Or rather, you can, but the moment will come when you must choose between them.

We were crossing the lot on our way to the coffins when suddenly Mary Ellen stamped her foot and cried,

"Lucky Strike!"

"What?"

"I stepped on a new one. See?"

So I stepped on it also.

"Lucky Strike."

She shook her head.

"You can say it if you want to, but it isn't as good as if you'd found your own. It counts less. And don't EVER step on a Pall Mall."

I felt a whole new mesh of complications engulf me.

"Let's not count cigarette packs. It's too hard."

I wanted her to tell me that in the scheme of things, Lucky Strikes and Pall Malls did not matter. Instead she only looked at me in astonishment.

"TOO HARD?"

"I can't remember so many things." I was beginning to feel irritable. "Why do we have to count things all the time? You keep track of license plates, you keep track of everything."

"It's only a game," she said in puzzled tones.

"Well, it isn't a game to me!" I bellowed.

The door of the funeral parlor opened and a man stepped out and cleared his throat. We scuttled across the lot to the street and began walking quickly past the houses toward downtown.

26

"A lot of people in there," whispered Mary Ellen, looking back over her shoulder. "You want to watch?"

"I don't want to watch anything any more! I'm tired of counting. All those things, I have to count them. I don't know why but I have to count them. And I don't want to. My head is so crowded with junk already that sometimes I feel like it's going to explode."

"Then why don't you quit?"

"I don't know!" My voice had risen to a shout. An old woman sitting on her front porch stared at us. "It's like there was some other person inside of me making me do it. Every time I want to quit there's that other person who won't let me."

Mary Ellen nodded.

"Somebody has put a hex on you, maybe," she suggested.

"Maybe," I agreed.

"If it happened to *me* I'd just go straight to Father Hekkel and he would make it all right."

The notion of involving a stranger alarmed me at once. Now that I'd dragged the thing into broad daylight it sounded foolish even to my own ears.

"Since you aren't in our church, maybe Father Hekkel wouldn't work. We better try and find somebody else."

"What about Abby?"

We were lucky. The only customer was white-haired Miss Briggs who worked in a dry goods store and looked like somebody's memory of a piano teacher. Miss Briggs was hunched under the dryer reading a confession magazine with the front cover folded back, and Abby was sweeping up the hair clippings that lay around the chairs into a feather pile.

Mary Ellen walked in and came right to the point.

"Anne-Marie has a devil in her."

"Lord-a-mighty!" cried Abby, nearly dropping the broom. "What makes you think so?"

And now I turned the light on my dark voices and told her everything, all my rituals from beginning to end, spewing them out like a bitter and humiliating confession. White horses and spilled salt and words that went cold on my tongue. The number of steps to the bedroom door and the long leap in the dark.

Abby listened gravely, glancing now and then at Miss Briggs who sat insulated by the hot rushing air like a silent and skinny warrior.

"Well," she said at last. "Well, well. A devil. Yes, indeed."

She did not seem to understand what we wanted of her, so Mary Ellen explained.

"We came to you because we thought you could call him out."

"Ah," said Abby, as calmly as if we'd asked her the time of day. "Well, I don't know the words for it. Go get that little black book over by the telephone."

Mary Ellen brought the book and Abby thumbed through it slowly. At last her finger paused on a page.

"Here are the words for the exorcizing of the devil."

She peered over her glasses, first at Mary Ellen and then at me. "A matter not to be taken lightly."

"No, of course not," I said, feeling myself in the presence of a great physician who would now perform a miraculous cure.

"If you're absolutely certain it's the devil, we ought to have the priest do this."

"I'd rather you did it, Abby."

Abby looked very pleased.

"Well then, you two stand behind that table."

Suddenly inspired, she went to the cupboard and took out the reliquary.

"There's nothing holier than the hucklebone of a saint."

She set it in the middle of the dressing table so that the mirror caught it from behind. Then she pushed Mary Ellen and me together, joining our hands on the relic as for a marriage, and laying the book open before her, she began to read in a loud voice.

I exorcize thee, most vile spirit, the very embodiment of our enemy, the entire specter, the whole legion, in the name of Jesus Christ, to get out and flee from this creature of God. He himself commands thee, who has ordered thee cast down from the heights of heaven to the depths of the earth. He commands thee, He who commands the sea, the winds, and the tempests. Hear, therefore and fear, O Satan, enemy of the faith, foe to the human race, producer of death, thief of life, destroyer of justice, root of evils, kindler of vices, procurer of sorrows. Why dost thou stand and resist, when thou knowest that Christ the Lord will destroy thy strength?

Under my grasp the hucklebone warmed. It had acquired for me a life of its own wholly different from its first life, just as it was Abby who read and yet not Abby but someone much older. Ancient, even. Not for Abby the beauty operator would the spirit of darkness depart but Abby the magician's daughter, daughter of Eve, last descendant of saint seekers and wanderers of holy places.

Her voice was rolling like thunder as she turned the page:

Now therefore depart. Depart, thou seducer. He expels thee, from whose eye nothing is secret. He expels thee to whose power all things are subject. He excludes thee, who has prepared for thee and thy angels everlasting hell; out of whose mouth the sharp sword will go, He who shall come to judge the quick and the dead and the world by fire.

"Too hot! Too hot!" shouted a voice, and we all yelled, and I thought I saw the devil in the mirror and shouted to Abby, but then he shrivelled into Miss Briggs making signs that she wanted to come out, forgetting, as the deaf do, that others can hear.

There was a snapping of hairpins as Abby pushed the dryer back and Miss Briggs emerged, as dazed as if she had awakened from a long sleep. Her hair lay against her scalp in crusted waves like cake frosting.

"What a funny color," observed Mary Ellen. "I believe your hair's darker than it was."

Miss Briggs sat down at the mirror and Abby took off the net and shook the pins loose. Nobody said a word for several minutes. Then Miss Briggs spoke up.

"It looks green," she whispered hoarsely. "Does it look green to you?"

Abby bent low for closer inspection, but you could have answered her just as well from across the room.

"It does have a sort of greenish cast. Sometimes a person can be allergic to the cream rinse."

"I never was before," said Miss Briggs, her face working.

Abby shook her head.

"I don't think a light rinse will cover it. You wouldn't want anything stronger than a rinse, would you?"

"Oh my, no. Just something to cover up the green."

"I could make it darker. Black, for example."

"Black!"

"It's better than green."

The silence prickled with voices. Why, Edith Briggs, what have you done to yourself? Would you believe it, running after the young men at her age?

Abby stuffed some change into my hand.

"Run downstairs and get two teas and some honey rolls."

Coming back we met Miss Briggs talking to herself on the stairs with her hair hanging black around her face in big rollers, like spaniel ears. Abby was nowhere in sight.

When I got home a palpable emptiness had invaded the house. Out of the dining room, with a rustling like blown

curtains, stepped Oskar. He had been sitting alone in the
falling light.

"They're all out looking for your grandmother," he said
brokenly. "She's run away. Slipped out of the house while
your ma was hanging up clothes."

"She couldn't have got very far," I said. "She has no
money."

"No. But she's a strong woman."

She was found about five blocks from the house, headed,
she believed, for the bus station. It had started to rain and the
drops glistened on her big sealskin coat and her white hair.
Mother hurried her upstairs and I heard the commotion of
bath water running and heaters being turned on that always
arose when I came home from school with wet feet.

"She'll catch cold, you wait and see," said Oskar, sorrow-
fully.

She could not go outside now but lay in her bed, swathed
in sweaters while the radiators pounded in her room and the
lights burned all night long. On the fourth day after her
flight she decided to get up. She seemed to have gathered
strength from her illness instead of losing it.

"I'll take her to market with me on Saturday," suggested
my father. "Better to take her out than to have her run off
again."

Market days were minor feast-days in our family. We
bought honey and vegetables to last us for the week and
sometimes such curiosities as acorn pipes and peacock feathers. Oskar and I would hold mock duels with our feathers
all week till they broke.

It was unseasonably brisk for May. The egg seller was
warming her feet at a tiny stove and the honey vendor had
incarcerated himself in a little hut with a plastic window,

behind which he waited as if for you to confess your sins. Grandmother walked among flats of pansies and beamed. For the first time that I could remember, she did not notice the cold.

She did not get up for church on Sunday but lay whispering quietly in bed, unaware even of the presence of the doctor, whose attentions would have been a welcome diversion in her hardier days.

"For pneumonia at her age, there's not much hope. You should take her to the hospital all the same; the oxygen facilities there will prolong her life a little."

"I want to have no regrets," said my mother. "It's so dreadful to have regrets afterwards."

My grandmother was put into a private room with nurses round the clock and a little cot near her bed for my mother, who told us how awful it would be to wake up at such a time and not know anybody.

But on Tuesday she was dead.

My mother came home from the hospital, her eyes ringed with blue. Neighbors brought in food, and casseroles, mostly chicken, began to accumulate in the kitchen. Suddenly plans for the funeral absorbed her with a thousand tedious details which ramified and consumed her grief. When Oskar stopped by our house that evening she ran up to him, eager and awkward, like a little girl.

"I don't know how I'm going to manage. Oskar, if you'd only stay. You could sleep on the sofa."

"Wouldn't it be easier to put me in Grandmother's room? I'd be out of the way."

My mother looked flustered.

"Do you think you'd be *comfortable* in there?"

I knew from her voice that she thought nobody could ever be comfortable there now.

"Well, well, we'll see," said Oskar.

His valise in the middle of the floor announced his decision. Keeping a wary eye on the open door, my mother stripped the bed with a studied casualness. Never had I heard her move so quietly, as if she were afraid of awakening the air itself. Suddenly the door slammed and she let out a shriek of terror.

Oskar rushed in.

"Let me do it," he said.

And I heard him plumping the pillows and humming tenderly to himself, straightening the bed, it seemed, for the woman who had recently left it.

Darkness fell so gently that nobody remembered to turn the lights on. We did not sit down for supper but picked at the casseroles spread out in the kitchen as for a church potluck. Oskar and my father, balancing paper plates on their knees, sat in the sun parlor, remembering death.

First Oskar remembered that the only extant photograph of his grandfather showed him in his coffin because Aunt Betty argued that a picture of him dead was better than no picture at all, and if you had the eyeballs touched in you could imagine him sitting in a first class railway carriage.

Then my father remembered the funeral of a young girl he attended during a diphtheria epidemic in which the mourners stood across the street and the coffin was tipped forward at the window by the girl's mother at a signal from the minister, who shouted his sermon from the front porch within hearing of both parties.

And then, in low voices, like children after the lights have been put down, they mused on the motions of the body after death. How hair and nails continue to grow and how the dead sit up in the furnace and their bones crack.

33

"You won't catch me being cremated," said Oskar. "When I'm down, I want to stay down."

At ten o'clock my father started the movement to bed. Last one up will be the first one dead—

I bit my tongue, remembering my newly won freedom, waited till the others had gone on ahead and then ascended the stairs. In my room I undressed quickly and started to jump into bed—

There is no one under the bed that will grab your feet.

I walked to the edge of the bed with slow and measured stride. Let the hands come if they dare. The body snatchers.

And then my mother's voice called out,

"Oskar, are you sure you won't be afraid in there?"

"Afraid?" His voice was filled with mild amazement. "Why should I be afraid? I loved the woman!"

His door closed but I heard him moving around, and a light under the crack spilled faintly into the hall. Presently he opened the door. The radiators were pounding. Mother had turned up the heat for Grandmother.

I got out of bed and stood in the doorway of my room and saw him, isolated in a little shell of light, as if I were looking at him through a mailing tube. He was sitting at the dressing table where Grandmother ate her breakfast, and he was writing calmly and steadily. I decided for no reason that he was writing a poem. On the back of a placemat, perhaps, or a menu, the surfaces which he preferred to write on above all else.

He did not see me. His back was turned and the light touched the thin places in his waistcoat with a soft shine. His habit of keeping his shoes on until the moment he stepped into bed gave him an air of expectancy at this hour; he would arise soon and go out for a visit or perhaps someone was coming to visit him. Suddenly I believed that if he turned out his light, every light in the world would go out. Then there would be no more left of him than the hucklebone of a saint.

When the sun came up his light disappeared. I was awakened by the sound of shoes dropping, and I dozed intermittently until I heard him shuffling quietly downstairs. There was a brief clatter in the kitchen and then the smell of coffee. I pulled on my clothes and went after him, trying to remember if my grandmother was already dead, if they had buried her yet, or if they would bury her today, but the only person I could find was Oskar. He poured me half a cup of coffee and filled the other half with milk.

"Do you want to take a little walk to the park?" he suggested. "Before anyone else gets up?"

We walked slowly past the teeter totters and sat down in the swings, though the seats were wet with dew. My uncle glided back and forth, trying to keep his swing even with mine, swinging without a word, as though the morning had turned him young again and he knew no more what had happened to Grandmother than I did.

GRAFFITO

Graffito

THE last train to the German border was leaving at sundown. When my mother and I arrived at the Bydgoszcz station, a great crowd was pushing its way toward the platform. There were baby buggies stuffed with carpets and sausages, there were dogs and soldiers, and children, hot and fierce in too many sweaters, all jostling each other in the calm dusty light that fell through the colored windows over the empty ticket office.

"Buy your ticket on the train, or you'll never make it to the border," shouted a man with no legs sitting in front of the counter.

My mother grabbed my hand and started running. Faces jammed the open windows of the train like a rogues' gallery. In the first car, a woman with a sack of potatoes on her back was blocking the door.

"Out of the way!" shouted the soldiers.

But she could not move. One of them split the sack down the middle with his bayonet and potatoes thundered to the floor, bumping under our feet. Suddenly a shriek of steam hid everything as the train began to move, very slowly, covered with people like roaches on a lump of sugar. My mother pushed me through the nearest window.

"Take care of yourself," she shouted. "We'll meet later."

Those inside lurched through the aisles, hunting for seats, stepping over the bundles and boxes, and the confusion gave way to a profound gratitude.

"If we had come a moment later! Only think—if we had stopped to pick up Ake's wife!"

I sat down next to an old woman who carried on her lap a wicker basket the right size for a cat. She kept her face turned toward the window, but against the darkening sky, her reflection seemed to fix me in a bleak stare. Then a dark-haired woman and a short man with a moustache sat down opposite us and wedged themselves in with an enormous bundle like a bruised hassock. Almost at once the woman set about rearranging the contents.

"Why bring butter? It will get rancid," said the man.

Instead of answering, she turned to me.

"Are you traveling alone?"

"No, my mother is riding somewhere on the train. We are from Tallin."

"Oh, there's a lot of people from Tallin here. But in the next car, they're all Poles." She wrinkled her nose. "Watch your things. The Poles steal."

Her husband held out a leather flask to the old woman by the window, who did not move.

"Beer," he said.

"It's warm," said his wife.

He shrugged and took a swallow himself.

"Let it go in the way it comes out."

Now she was pulling out a number of scrolls, canvases that snapped open like springs when she touched them. A general in a black uniform and the head of an elegant woman flashed past before she rolled them all into a single tube.

"When we go back, after the war, we'll have them reframed."

"Your passports, please! Get your passports ready!"

A soldier was pushing his way down the aisle. The old woman at the window gave a violent twitch and rummaged through her jacket. Behind us, people were standing and opening valises. I realized quite suddenly that I had no passport. But when the soldier came to our seat, he leaned over and said very slowly in German,

"Your mother says to you, don't worry. She is riding on the outside of the train."

I did not understand.

"Has she got a seat?" I asked.

He pointed to the doorway.

"She's riding out there. When we cross the border, a lot of people will have to get off."

I followed him to the platform, and a strong wind slammed the door after us. Over the jagged profiles of men in caps and a few stolid old women, the stars rocked like light on stirred water. The train joggled and lurched. I looked again at the women and saw my mother, hanging on to the doorway with her arms pulled out behind her. When I had seen her, I returned to my seat.

"Did you find her?" asked the dark-haired woman.

I nodded.

"She's riding outside."

"Outside! It is very cold to be riding there."

In the darkness, silence settled like dust on us all. The towns flew by invisibly and it furred the roofs, the vast fields, and the milky edges of morning. I slept fitfully through the clatter of wheels and saw my mother riding on the sea like a broken figurehead, then saw her wash ashore in a summer out of early childhood, a confusion of farms and sky.

"Wake up—we're coming to the border!"

41

My mother was pressing her cold hands against my cheeks and my eyes flew open.

"Give her some beer, Ivo. How cold you are! Give her your seat."

The dark-haired woman was rubbing my mother's arms, curiously freckled with light. Her skin seemed to breathe cold.

"No beer? Water, then. Here, you—" she thrust a little tin cup at me.

In the toilet at the end of the car, I found a rat, its head crushed, behind the door. There was no more water. But over the sink someone had written in German simple enough even for me to read,

If I had my way, I would not have married him. For Hans has gone to Chernigov and all my people, alas, are dead.

 THE BOY

WHO RAN

WITH

THE DOGS

The Boy
Who Ran with the Dogs

E USED to dream of taming a dog that didn't be-
long to anyone, a dog with no bell. How sometimes they would meet and he would bring it a
little food, the dog waiting at a safe distance,
and then one day the dog would follow him. He always saw
himself in the green costume that people wore when they
tamed animals. Because whenever he lay in bed, thinking
about the dog he would tame, he saw very clearly in the
dark a man in such a costume surrounded by a circle of white
horses, a wheel with the man at the center. The boy was not
sure if he had ever seen such a thing or not; it seemed to him
he had seen it once long ago in a circus, but he could not be
certain, and he did not want to ask his mother for fear she
would say it was not true.

In the morning he hardly heard the jingle of bells that kept
him awake at night. He walked down the road to the beach
every day by himself, with its colored umbrellas, and every
family had its dog, brought here for the summer. He would
spread out his small striped towel and warm himself in the
sun and watch the clusters of families, thinning out now as
the summer was ending, and in the evening after dinner he
walked along the beach, noticing how far down on an empty
stretch of sand the dogs would be running together, two or
three, snarling over a stick, some wearing bells which would

drop off as the salt water gnawed through their collars and left them free.

"It's a crime how so many people go away and leave them to run," said his mother. "They haven't the heart to shoot them, but they let them starve to death."

That made him sad, though he always felt sad when the summer people left, closing up their cottages for the season so that he felt that he had been left behind with the handful of families that lived on all year round in this place. Now he wanted to leave food out for the dogs, but his mother said no, wasn't it bad enough that they should be running in packs up and down the street at night, so that you could hardly step out your door to mail a letter without running into them? And wasn't it bad enough that a child had already been bitten and treated for rabies, because no one could find the dog and if anyone had found it, no one would claim it?

Sitting on his striped towel among the umbrellas that were very sparse now because of the wind, he wondered how any creature could live alone. If his mother turned him out, where would he go? He saw himself walking along a road, then decided he would make a little house under his grand-father's porch to keep himself out of the rain, sleeping under one of the rowboats the old man stored there for the summer people. Cats always used to go under the porch; in a rain-storm you could see them brooding like hens. But cats were always a little bit stray to begin with, never really giving themselves to people, so it would be easier for them than for him. They were never really owned, never went to the beach with families and shared the umbrella and the frankfurter scraps with fathers and mothers and children, or fetched sticks from the water, or went to the place where they had done all these things, waiting patiently for the family that never came back.

Sometimes he had dinner with his grandfather and there would be a message from his mother which the old man kept to himself until it was time to go home, and then just as the boy was about to leave, he would say, looking not at the boy but off in another direction,

"Your mother won't be home tonight and says you're to stay here with me."

Though the boy always followed his grandfather into the house, he felt a great longing to go home at once, which never lasted more than a few minutes but turned into a gnawing curiosity to know what his mother was doing. He knew that she did not work all night, because when he cut across the wet fields in the morning to his house, his mother had already left for the diner. No matter how early he got up, he could not find out the truth of this thing. He would dress himself quickly, tiptoe through the house and open the front door, only to hear his grandfather behind him suddenly, inexplicably, calling him back.

"Surely you're not going away without breakfast."

Then he would come back and they would sit down together. The old man would bring on pancakes and orange juice and syrup ready as if by magic, which he would eat slowly, remarking on the weather—it would be a dry fall, a good hunting season—until the boy's impatience dissolved in the hopelessness of his own ineptitude.

He wished he were invisible and could run very fast, straight to the diner. Through the steamed-up windows he could see his mother, pushing her yellow hair behind her ears, leaning over to wipe the crumbs off the counter, leaving a trail of water beads which she wiped again, talking to the truck drivers and hunters hunched around her, not as she talked to him over their late supper. More as if she were singing.

47

"Why Missus McCallister, I didn't know you had a boy as old as this one!"

He could have gone inside, as he had done that day, but ever since he had felt funny about it, as if his mother had told him not to. So he would watch them from outside, with the sound turned off, and he would write with his finger on the window to tell her he was here.

His grandfather's cabin was cosier than his own house, he thought, though barer, since the room he slept in had no collections of things like his bedroom at home. His grandfather laughed when he told about the eggshells and the nests.

"Why do you save eggshells?"

The boy didn't know why, really. He didn't particularly like birds, in fact, he hardly knew the names of any of them, though he liked to watch them fly through the tall trees, never hitting a branch. Sometimes he thought it was because they lived in the air and hardly anyone ever saw them up close. That was what made the shells he found in the forest more valuable than the eggshell of a hen, though it might be speckled as pleasantly as the thrush's or dove's.

At night the boy heard animals in the trees outside the cabin, the footfall of bear and deer, the running of dogs.

"No bears so close to the houses as this," said his grandfather. "And likely no deer, either. Probably the dogs."

When he stood in the woods, he thought he could hear their bells, even in the daytime. Once somebody's cows had wandered in from the other side, but the bells he listened for did not click like theirs, heavy and slow as churchbells. But that was in midsummer. By now the dogs must have lost their collars.

They were bolder now, coming into town to ravage the garbage pails, running down the streets where once they trotted at their owners' heels, named and clipped and loved.

Under his grandfather's porch, where he had once watched cats, the boy put a plateful of bread and bones. Then he sat down on the top step alone to wait.

At twilight they came, slowly, the dogs he had seen all summer on the beach, shaggy and bigger now, though thinner, having the shapes of rabbits, of deer, moving with the caution of wild things. They fixed him with their eyes, as if enraged, then slunk past him and began tearing at the bread and bones. From the step he could hear their breathing underneath him, their grunting and faint snarling over the bigger bones, the scraping and mashing of bones against teeth. Only when they were gone did he remember that one dog, a cheap imitation of an Irish setter, had eaten nothing but watched him with yellow eyes the entire time.

As soon as his mother sent for him, he would go to the diner and tell his mother he needed some food. *For yourself? No, for some friends of mine. A couple of chops will do? A string of franks? I got to ask the cook. Oh, Missus McCallister, you know any friends of the boy are friends of mine.*

He went every night to the porch now, huddling in the darkness while a few yards off his grandfather sat in his room and polished his guns; the boy sat just outside the circle of light that lay on the ground by the window. Now he came not only to watch the dogs tear at the food he carried to them but to wait for those who returned later to sleep, going round and round, as if beating down centuries of grass, the way the most civilized dogs will do, laying their noses delicately on their shaggy paws.

When they had settled themselves for sleep, he went down into their darkness, laying his head on his knees, feeling on his skin the warm breath of poodles, woolly and burred, crippled setters whose legs had mended the wrong way with no one to set them, great Danes and spaniels, and the children of one breed by another till you wouldn't know what name to give them. They did not growl but nudged close against him, to keep him warm, he thought, though when they yawned in the darkness he could see their great teeth shining, hard but curiously gentle, like sprouts growing in a cellar that bend at a touch.

I can get you better than bones and bread. My mother will give me chops and franks if I ask her to. And where is your mother? She's waiting to send for me. And what will you do when she sends for you? I'll go to the park and sit on a bench. No it wasn't a park, it was a big field—he was not sure suddenly exactly where they walked together so long ago but he went bravely on—with lots of animals in it. *Dogs? No, no, horses and elephants and a lion. And your father? My father wears a green costume and leads the horses around*—it wasn't true, he thought fearfully, and yet perhaps it was his father by this time. *And when will you go to your mother? When she sends for me.*

Now in the evening when the dogs ran he ran with them. They padded silently through the streets, he at a loping trot, sometimes pausing to open the lid of a garbage pail so that the dogs could tear the paper bags, soaked through with coffee grounds, and the crusts and scraps of gristle, taking none for himself but remembering as he saw these things spilling out on gravel and sidewalks that he sometimes sat at a table and his people threw out the crusts and the scraps that kept the dogs alive.

The next morning he let himself in at the window, lifting out the little screen and setting it on the floor inside, then scrambling over the low sill. He lay down on his bed, careful not to rumple it, for he did not know how to make a bed and always slept on top of the spread when he stayed with his grandfather. Now he did not sleep but listened to birds waking in pairs here and there; occasionally a whole thicket of them woke up at once, as if frightened by a cat. At last he tiptoed out of bed and opened the front door, waiting for his grandfather's voice to call out, like a hand at the scruff of his neck,

"Surely you're not going away without breakfast!"

Then they would sit down together and the pancakes would begin to sizzle, and the old man would motion his grandson to eat, heaping his plate with cakes like silver dollars and water lily pads and hotwater bottles, promising that he could fry his initials on the griddle with the last of the batter. But the boy had no appetite. His eyes smarted from lack of sleep, and he felt drugged and sullen, trying to keep awake at the table. On the clean white plates, the cakes and butter tasted pasty and dead.

Sometimes when he sat at the table it seemed he saw two grandfathers that never appeared at the same time but rather quivered on the verge of one turning into the other. There was the grandfather who smelled of tobacco and wool and peeled sticks, and there was the man who smelled faintly sticky sweet and very cold, and sat in a pool of light like a moth, polishing his gun as if he had morning and night strung up in a bag for dinner.

It was not the first time a man looked so strange to him. He was running with the dogs on a hill, fierce with gooseberry and mock orange and lilacs, all past the time of their blooming, touched with the first yellow of fall, when he saw light just beyond it. Someone had cut the shrubs to look like turrets, the grass was very smooth, with chairs white-slatted like picket fences and a picnic table where two men and two women were sitting. Beside one of the women he could see a little boy, about as tall as himself, and for a moment he had the queer feeling that the woman was his mother and he had been replaced. He stood in the darkness looking at the women in shrill prints and the men in their short-sleeved shirts; he remembered the naked look of their arms. One of the men stepped very close to him and lit a glass lamp on a tall post, so that black smoke angled toward the underbrush.

"That'll fix the mosquitoes."

"I have some 6–12," said a woman. "It always works."

The man went over to a small grill and held up a string of sausages and looked right at him without seeing him.

"Anyone for seconds?"

The setter gave a low growl and everyone froze. One of the women lifted her head.

"What was that?"

"I didn't hear anything."

"Oh, I did."

The man moved to the edge of the light, being very careful not to trespass outside. He peered out and saw nothing, not the eyes or the waiting or the hunger.

"There's nobody here."

Then a shriek from the woman:

"Look there."

He had stepped too close, he was in the light. The man whirled and lunged but the boy was not there, he was running with the dogs behind and ahead of him, leaving the man to grope in the wilderness at the edge of his land. Their voices followed him.

"It was the dogs."

"Enormous—they're getting bigger."

"By winter they'll attack us in our homes."

When my mother sends for me, you can all come and live in my room.

"I heard them last night; they're very close to us, I think," said his grandfather. He was making a sundial, hammering a square of wood to the fork of a birch trunk, cut off just below the outbreak of smaller branches.

"Who is close to us?"

"The dogs."

The boy was anxious to leave but found he could not take his eyes from his grandfather's hands as they straightened the square with its painted numerals and poised the nails and struck them, one by one, into the soft birch.

"The sheriff put a bounty on them—ten dollars a head, a hundred for the pack."

"Are they worth as much as that?" cried the boy, astonished.

His grandfather shrugged.

"Tried to kill a baby."

The boy sat down, suddenly very cold.

"It was the mother's fault for leaving it alone in the yard. In broad daylight it happened."

"All the dogs did it?"

"No. One or two, I think. But what does it matter? Any one of them could have done it."

And his grandfather began to speak of the danger, of how nobody walked around these days without a bit of lead pipe or a flashlight to shine into a dog's eyes and blind him. People were burning all their garbage now and those with outhouses locked them at night for fear the dogs would turn them over, and a few were spreading stories of werewolves with some skepticism but some fear also.

But even as he was speaking, the boy thought he heard them coming, slinking through the darkness under the porch, beating down the invisible grass and lying with their heads on their paws, waiting for him.

In the morning the boy got up early, tiptoed into the living room, opened the front door, and found to his astonishment that nobody called him back. He waited for someone to tell him what to do; then he remembered the fields he had not yet crossed to his mother's house; then he looked up and saw his grandfather.

He was striding through the woods, having crossed the fields wet with morning, and he carried a suitcase.

"I've been to see your mother," he exclaimed, plopping wearily down on the steps. "She says you're to stay with me for a little while. She hasn't been well, you know—"

The boy tried to look grave.

"I think I got everything you'll need for a while," said the old man. "Even your—"

He snapped open the suitcase and lifted out a shoe box, squeezed shut with a rubber band around it.

"—your eggshells and nests."

She did not send for him. Why did she not send for him? She was very ill, lying in a white bed in a white room in the middle of the house—he suddenly thought, but we have no white rooms in that house, and he knew she would be lying in a room with flowers on the wallpaper. *If I am invisible and can run very fast, I can run to my mother's house.*

With the dogs he knew he was invisible.

Has she sent for you, then?

The house was very dark. *Maybe your mother is walking in the fields with your father?* They took the hill by stealth and walked around the house. The shades were drawn in the living room and the rooms upstairs. The boy stood on his toes and peered into the kitchen and saw the clock on the stove gleaming; you could see its numbers in the dark. And that other gleam—was that the toaster or what?

He continued on around to the back yard. Someone had left the lawn mower in the middle of the grass, having mowed about a quarter of the small lawn. The day lilies and forsythia bush he could not see.

And whose black car was this in the driveway? His mother had no car.

Then upstairs a light flashed on, and against the shade he could see someone, his mother moving—no, two people, or was it one? Almost immediately it went off again, and a man's voice called out,

"Who's there?"

The child did not answer. He wanted to call out and ask his mother to please send for him soon, but perhaps this was not his mother. He knew she was not his mother until she sent for him.

When he reached his grandfather's house, he did not let himself in the window. He stood on the porch, looking through the trees toward the fields he had just crossed while the dogs sniffed his legs and turning past him, disappeared among the shapes of rowboats, panting lightly; their teeth flashed in the darkness. Softly the boy crept after them, huddled in the air that seemed to breathe by itself with the pulsing of so many bodies. Now when he touched their necks he could not tell where the collars had been; the fur had all grown over.

We came too soon. Too soon for the chops and sausages. We came at night, that was wrong, we should have come in the morning—he thought suddenly, but why was it wrong?

Dozing among the lumps and snouts of the dogs, he felt their tongues dripping against his wrists and face, a brimming of hidden springs.

He did not know what woke him, unless it was the dogs all lifting their heads at once, the way swimmers rise to the surface of a lake. The delicate nostrils quivered. The boy did

55

not know the smell of danger, yet he felt the heaviness of another presence outside near them.

"Grandfather?" he whispered.

"Don't move!" cried his grandfather's voice. "Don't move!"

The boy jerked himself awake, striking his head on the rim of a boat. In the entrance to the shelter he saw his grandfather crouching like an enormous spider. The gleam of the muzzle quivered; the old man pointed it to the left of the boy, toward the ground.

Behind him the light was breaking. The child could not see his grandfather's face, but the sun caught every hair on the old man's head and set it aflame.

"Don't be afraid," shouted another voice that the boy did not know.

"Are you all right?"

When he did not answer, the shape in the doorway fired once, twice, four times, each explosion pumping the air with smoke, striking the boy's ears like a knife. All around him he heard the quick whines and silences of the dogs, and he pressed himself further back among the boats, terrified.

"It's all right now, it's all right—" shouted his grandfather in a huge trembling voice, and the boy felt rough hands tugging at him, and he clung like a barnacle.

Then his nails slipped, bringing up splinters and paint as the old man lifted him out, and he tried to push the rough tweed jacket away from his face.

"Set him down, set him down," said the other man's voice.

As he uncrumpled himself and landed on his feet, he saw his mother reach out her arms to take him, but she looked wholly strange to him now with her coat thrown over her as if in anger and her blonde hair pushed back behind her ears. With a wild cry he clasped hold of his grandfather's legs, stumbling after him, so that he should not see the sheriff bringing out the bodies of the dogs and he began to bawl into his own sleeve that smelled of the dogs and their matted fur and the smell of his grief.

THE BEAUTIFUL SUNDAY

The Beautiful Sunday

THE taxi was half an hour late, and I was in a panic. The train for Mont-St.-Michel left, according to my mimeographed instructions, in about five minutes. "To the Gare Montparnasse," I shouted. I opened the door for myself and leaping into the back seat jostled a woman in a plastic rain bonnet who crackled when she moved.

The driver threw up his hands.

"There is no train leaving from Gare Montparnasse," he shouted back. "There is a strike, Madame. All the trains in Paris stop for thirty-six hours."

The woman leaned forward and pointed to her instructions, identical to mine, except that she had carefully penciled in a translation: *The Beautiful Sundays. Departure of the Special Train at midnight from Station Montparnasse, arrive at the Station of Pontorson six a.m.*

"From Montparnasse," she urged. "You see, it says here."

The driver looked at us both accusingly, made a surly noise deep in his throat, and roared away without another word. The woman introduced herself to me as Mrs. Pierce.

To the satisfaction of the driver, the station was empty and completely dark, except for a faint glow coming from the far side. I got out and paid him without looking at his face and started toward it, listening to the ring of Mrs. Pierce's heels on the cement until I saw a Chinese porter who hurried smoothly past us as if on castors.

"The trains," said Mrs. Pierce, sleeving him. "Where are the trains?"

"There are no trains," he said wearily.

"*Les Beaux Dimanches*," I added.

"Ah!" He seemed about to smile but did not. "Follow me."

He led us to the only outgoing train in Paris. The light we had seen was here on the platform.

"Not very many people, are there?" said Mrs. Pierce. "Unless they're all sitting in the dark. What number is your car?"

"Twenty-four."

We began to count the numbers, which ran alternately eleven, thirteen, fifteen, seventeen, nineteen, twenty-one, twenty-three. Mrs. Pierce frowned.

"Perhaps they're numbered differently on the other side."

Behind us a few people in uniform were wandering about, and I approached one of them.

"Numéro twenty-four?"

Together we counted the cars again. The man chattered rapidly with a few of his cronies, then turned to us and shrugged.

"Numéro twenty-four—*n'existe pas.*"

"What!" exclaimed Mrs. Pierce. "But we have our tickets."

"Try numéro twenty-three," he suggested, and waved us away.

Inside, the train was very chilly and so dark that I could not see the numbers of the compartments. It hardly mattered, since the first three were locked. But the fourth opened with a clatter, and two figures started up quickly.

"Excuse me—may we sit here?"

"*Mais oui!* What number is your seat?" The spryest one

seized my ticket and bent it toward the window. "You are in car twenty-four. This is car twenty-three."

"Car twenty-four doesn't exist," said Mrs. Pierce.

"It doesn't exist? *Mon Dieu*! In that case—"

Magnanimously, she gestured us to sit down, I next to her, Mrs. Pierce next to a white-haired woman in a heavy grey coat that gave her the shape of a dormouse.

Before the silence could grow awkward, the door jerked open and a couple appeared, striking matches and squinting at the seat numbers. A huge leather purse struck my knee.

"I never heard of such a thing," exclaimed a woman's voice. "I have my ticket for car twenty-four. I bought it a month ago, in this very station."

"And so did these people," said the woman next to me.

"Are there so few of us going?" exclaimed the man. He peered hopelessly into the gloom, then seated himself opposite Mrs. Pierce, bumping his head against the high back.

And now no one spoke at all. Mrs. Pierce uncrumpled her instructions, which she had kept in her glove, and studied them carefully by the dim light from the platform, following her translation with one finger.

When the train arrives, render yourself on the place found in the proximity of the station in order to take your place on board the bus effecting the transfer between Pontorson and Mont-St.-Michel. This transfer will be effected by the bus in two rotations with a stop for breakfast (three francs, included).
The day is free to permit you to assist in the different manifestations.
Departure of the special train from Pontorson is at five o'clock.
With the box lunch for dinner (ten francs, included), you will be remitted a consummation of your choice.
We wish you an agreeable journey.

"It's going to be a long day," she observed. "What are the manifestations?"

The train lurched forward and from outside the window we heard a confused buzzing. Around the corner of the station a large crowd of people came running toward us. The lights in the compartment flashed on and we stared at each other curiously.

"Well!" said the man. "It seems I am alone here."

The woman next to me began to fan herself with a thickly folded map, on the corner of which was printed in a neat schoolgirl hand, "Marie Giot." Then she turned to me.

"You are English?"

"English," I said.

"American," said Mrs. Pierce.

The man, seeing something was expected of him, said quickly, "French."

"French?"

"French—from St. Petersburg."

"*Pardon!*" exclaimed Madame Giot. "I thought you were German."

The dormouse in her grey coat looked at each of us through her thick lenses, put her hand to her mouth and smiled.

All at once the crowd invaded the car, tramping noisily up and down the aisles, opening the doors, excusing themselves or scrambling eagerly for seats. Somewhere, the heat rumbled on. The man from St. Petersburg took a small parcel and held it to his nose.

"There's no reason," he said to his wife, "why it ought to leak."

And now the ancient creature in the corner who had hardly uttered a word let out a little shriek.

"*Fermez! Fermez!*" she shouted at Mrs. Pierce.

"What?" said Mrs. Pierce.

But Madame Giot climbed deftly over us and slammed the door.

"In the next compartment, there is a mouse."

It was two in the morning when we left Paris.

The seat, thinly upholstered and perfectly straight, pushed against the small of my back; I dreamed fitfully of being in church. The train jogged me back, over and over, to the close darkness of the car, until I opened my eyes and saw through the window a milky haze rising from the fields outside. Madame Giot shook me eagerly when she saw me awaken.

"Look," she said, wiping a hole in the mist on the glass, "we are approaching Brittany."

I looked out on an endless stretch of tall grass in which the small houses seemed to be kneeling. Cows pushed slowly across the pastures, sleepy and oddly weightless, as if underwater.

"It's a beautiful place," she mused. "My husband was from Brittany. From Quimper. He was a most beautiful man. During the war he went to Canada. Ah, look—there's a church. It's very old, you know."

The discovery of the houses, churches and small towns gave her a keen delight, as if she knew them from before.

"You've been to Mont-St.-Michel already, have you?" I inquired.

"No," she said. "But I've been to the exposition in Paris. It was marvellous. There was a little replica, done to scale, of the Abbey."

The others began to stretch themselves, waking to the strong smell of liverwurst. Unabashed, the old woman in the corner was unwrapping a hard flat sandwich from the bottom of her purse and tearing off chunks with her teeth, smacking noisily.

Mrs. Pierce took out a cigarette, held it in her mouth for a moment, looked round at us all, and put it back in her pocket. Light broke above the hills outside.

"It seems to me," said the man from St. Petersburg, after a long silence, "that the breakfast is very late."

We arrived at Pontorson at six in the morning and got off at a small station decorated with geranium boxes. Next door stood a café, also decorated with geraniums. Both faced a strip of uncut grass which separated an orchard and tiny vegetable garden from the tracks.

"How will we get to the Mount?" asked the old woman, more to herself than to any of us.

I glanced down at Mrs. Pierce's translation.

This transfer will be effected by the bus in two rotations with a stop for breakfast.

It took eight rotations, not two. Some stopped for coffee in the café, which was wholly unprepared for this party of three hundred people. The owner hastily whisked the chairs from the table tops where he had stacked them the night before. A few latecomers sat hunched on the terrace, chilly and damp, for there was a fine mist in the air that glistened like rain on coats and faces. Madame Giot passed them all without a qualm and headed for the bus.

"I can wait," she said. "I want to arrive in time for Mass."

We ate our breakfast at long tables in an enormous dining room while four young girls raced back and forth with pots of coffee and baskets of bread, brittle as coral. Across from me, the man from St. Petersburg revived at the sight of the bread and butter.

"Milk here," he said, holding up the pitcher. "Who wants milk?"

"Two francs for the coffee, one for the milk, one franc for the bread, one franc for butter, that's five francs. And they only charged us three!" His wife was triumphant. "It's a real bargain."

"Doesn't it remind you of a family reunion?" exclaimed Madame Giot, fiercely pulling a piece of bread in two.

The restaurant was full of gladiolas in silver vases crowded along the bar across the room. On a sideboard three feet from our table, someone had carefully arranged bottles of dressing and a tray of cheese wedges wrapped in gold foil. There was a milk glass pitcher, showing in relief a procession of saints, which held an arrangement of red carnations. Mrs. Pierce, smelling strongly of wet plastic, nudged my arm.

"I wonder who that's for?"

The old woman from our compartment raised her lip slightly, baring yellow teeth.

"It's not for the likes of us."

The bus to the Mount was silent with attentive watchers. Straddling a folding seat in the aisle, I looked past rows of shoulders and heads down the narrow road, very straight and lined with poplars. It seemed to end abruptly in a dazzling emptiness. And because we were all looking so intensely ahead of us, no one realized, for half a minute, that the crown and spire of the city was rising over the hill to the left, only to drop from view and reappear as we turned a corner. Clearly the road ended at Mont-St.-Michel.

"How sudden it is!" cried a voice.

"It's that way with all the great churches," whispered Madame Giot. "Chartres is the same. You look up and see it standing in the midst of a wheat field."

"The sun is coming out!"

Suddenly there were no more trees. On all sides of us the white tidal plain spread flat and smooth, stretching far off to the glittering suggestion of sea. And inescapably present, the

67

island and the city confronted us, enormous and fragile, bone-colored in the fog, like some ancient ceremonial flask, hollowed perhaps by the sea but finished by man.

After the first astonishment everyone resumed chattering.

"When the tide comes in, are we trapped?"

"No, it doesn't cover the road. Some people want the road taken away, so you could reach the mount only by boat. That would be better, don't you think?"

The bus drew up to the gate and parked at the foot of the wall. The loneliness of the city, in which nothing stirred, and the vast desert around it reminded me of what I used to imagine the moon would feel like, if a man were allowed to walk there. Who, after all, lives on Mont-St.-Michel? I thought. For when we passed through the gate, we entered the dead city, or at least a living museum, which is nearly the same thing.

One woman, hearing the crowd, was opening her shop, bringing out a tray of postcards and ceramic plates painted with primitive figures in Breton costumes. The rest of the town remained closed, a city of stone, damply gleaming after the morning shower. A few lingered to buy; the rest of us climbed the broad winding stairway to the church. A man in a black raincoat, like a spy, was holding the door open, and we thronged in, shuffling our feet, shaking the drops from ourselves like dogs. Madame Giot frowned at the commotion.

"The monastery is still in use, I think."

If it was, there was no sign of the monks, and we allowed ourselves to be pushed slowly through a series of draughty passages into the sanctuary. Stripped of all furnishings, it had the look of a place recently pillaged, from which the people had fled.

"Oh!" said the woman from St. Petersburg, "where are the colored windows?"

But these too were gone. Passing the small modern crucifix hanging near the entrance, she crossed herself vaguely.

"You are Catholic?" asked Madame Giot.

"I used to be."

Far away at the other end of the room, the guide in the black raincoat was shouting about the splendors of the altarpiece which, alas, had been destroyed. His voice bounced from wall to wall as he paced up and down, showing how the monks came here, knelt here, how the statue of Saint Michael stood there, and how the pilgrims gathered here, on litters, on crutches, waiting to be cured.

"They came by the thousands," he said, "like you."

There was a polite ripple of laughter. Then he hurried us off to the cloisters, a stone gallery of sand-colored arches, paned with glass, which seemed to hang high over the desert. Brilliant patches of moss clung to the stone where water trickled thinly out of the cracks. It smelled like a spring morning.

"Damn," said Mrs. Pierce suddenly, as she stooped to retrieve a package from the floor. "Somebody stepped on my plate." She shook it. "Broken."

When we came out the town was awake, the sun warm and clear in the sky. The walls seemed to have folded away into hundreds of little shops, hung with nets and knives, jugs, barometers, gargoyles, skulls, bells, copper pots, sailor's caps, and the little silver shells that pilgrims buy to wear in their own cities. Saints, glazed yellow and blue, hung in bunches like Spanish onions, and the open doors were beaded with ceramic bowls showing, in a ribbon-like script, the most popular names: Yves, Jacques, Marie, Anne, Pierre. People thronged the shops, fingering the masks, the anchors, the shells packed with marzipan, the holy medals. Carrying their coats, they jostled each other in lines and waited for crêpes, lifted from the raw pile limp as a rag and fried crisp before their very eyes, and sprinkled with fine sugar.

On the stairs leading to the church, a man was setting up a tripod and a very large camera, so that he would be ready for the procession, he explained, which he was photographing for an American television show.

"I'm staying with him," said Mrs. Pierce. "Who would know better than a photographer what's the best view of things?"

Madame Giot was bustling through the crowd toward me, from one of the lower chapels.

"Have you been to Mass?" she smiled radiantly. "I have. It is wonderful."

The procession was a curious and rapid affair. There was a band from one of the neighboring towns—for Mont-St.-Michel has few indigenous children and could never have assembled a group of schoolboys like these, in blue smocks and black broad-brimmed hats, marching irreverently down the cobbled street and playing their bagpipes. The crowd waited but nothing further appeared, and the American photographer started to fold up his equipment. A priest, perspiring heavily, rushed to stop him.

"Wait," he urged, "here comes the rest of it."

Sure enough, several young women were walking to the traces of music far ahead of them, dressed in tall white *coiffes* and the heavily embroidered velvets commonly found in Victorian piano shawls. The queen of the festival smiled a gap-toothed smile, and with a flutter of tasselled banners, they all disappeared into the church. I felt a wave of disappointment.

"They'll be by again—I don't want to sit through any services," said Mrs. Pierce. "Let's see what's around back."

At the foot of the wall, just outside the city, the tide was coming in, and a small group had gathered on the rocky slope to watch it. Two Japanese photographers were sunning themselves decorously on the smooth slab, their shoes resting neatly on an adjacent boulder. The man from St. Petersburg and his wife had opened a box of figs and were throwing the stems over their shoulders. Chewing vigorously, she was turning the pages of a magazine spread out on her lap.

"There's no reason," he said, "for the box to leak."

When he saw us coming, he folded the lid down and graciously invited us to join them. Mrs. Pierce removed her plastic rain hat for the first time, and I took off my shoes, which were full of small stones and covered with dust.

"We have the best view in the world," he grumbled, "and my wife reads a magazine. She goes to Mont-St.-Michel and buys a magazine because it has Nureyev on the cover. Have you seen Nureyev?"

"No," I said, "but he's very good."

"But not so good as Nijinsky," said the man.

He looked down from our rock at a party of nuns who were throwing stones into the water, trying to make them skip.

"Nobody remembers Nijinsky anymore. But I saw him once when he was an old man. He was living in Poland then, crazy as a loon. I was with the division that came through his town. The captain went from house to house, asking for quarters, and when the wife handed him their papers, he said, 'It's not the same Nijinsky? Here, in Poland?' But it was. And the whole division brought him flowers and made a fire outside his house, and the old man came out and danced with us. Sixty years old he was—it was magnificent."

The real life of the city, I decided, went on in the shadow

of its walls, which not only surrounded but labyrinthed it inside, shaping the city unobtrusively, like a skeleton under the ragged ivy and the secret courtyards, each with its cats and laundry and vegetable garden. Goldenrod, buttercups, honeysuckle covered the walls of the Abbey gardens, lilac, wild iris—all this, waiting out of sight. And from these passages and these courtyards, one could look out on the cobbled road that led to the church and watch the people streaming up and down the mountain or standing at the top, watching the tide come in.

"The wonder is," said Madame Giot, picking the burrs off her skirt, "that it has survived."

We were waiting for the train at Pontorson, some sitting on the asphalt platform, some at the café, while others had crossed the tracks and spread their coats on the grass at the end of the orchard. The sun was hanging in a low cage of branches. The old woman stood gazing hard up the track, her coat slung heavily on her arm, as if she could draw the train forward with the ferocity of her stare.

"If the train arrives after midnight, I shall miss the last métro to St. Denis."

The woman from St. Petersburg was still reading her magazine and pointing out some pictures to her husband.

"The soul!" he exclaimed. "Would you believe it? Here it shows photographs of the human soul."

We all leaned over to look. There were two photographs, all black save for some smoky areas, like an X-ray. The old woman gave a cackle.

"What does it say?"

"It says, 'Maurice Maeterlinck, for all his writings, felt that his greatest achievements were these photographs of the soul of Mary Garden.' "

"*Mon Dieu!*" cried Madame Giot, appalled.

Then a group of people not far from us scrambled to their feet and we heard the train, and everyone rushed across the track to take their places in the coach.

But it was not easy to leave the mount. We watched the steeple of the church dwindle into the trees and I thought we had seen the last of it, until Madame Giot sprang up with a shout,

"The steeple! I see it!"

Sure enough, it showed itself for a few moments, then swung away and came up in a different spot.

"We are taking the circular route," she exclaimed, "through Normandy."

Then we saw something shining on the horizon and the old lady thought it was the sea; but it was the steeple, which hovered above the trees like the smallest needle before it twinkled out of sight.

"That's the end," said Madame Giot, content. Her eye fell on the round parcel which the woman from St. Petersburg held on her lap. "I see you bought a plate."

The woman nodded in surprise. "Did you buy nothing?"

"Oh, yes," said Madame almost shyly, "for my collection —look."

Carefully she took from her wallet a block of four postage stamps, showing the angel of Mont-St.-Michel.

It was almost too dark to see them, in the falling sunlight which covered everything with a fiery haze. Outside the window, young cows were running terrified beside the train. Women paused in the fields to watch us pass, rising up from the low stools where they sat milking.

"They have forgotten the dinner," said the old lady sadly.

Mrs. Pierce reached into her purse and pulled out an apple. "You may have this, if you like. I've got another."

She took it with a smile, held it for awhile in her hand, and then slipped it quietly into her bag.

Nobody turned the lights on, and we sat, each absorbed in his own silence, as the train rolled into Paris. The seats had made my back stiff again, and I was eager to get off. From all over the car there was the sound of people stumbling to their feet, or packages being assembled. The station was bustling with people; an efficient voice called out the numbers of the trains and their arrivals and departures.

Hoping to be among the first to leave, the couple from St. Petersburg had gone to wait in the corridor. Mrs. Pierce was hunting for her rainhat under the seat. I shook hands with Madame Giot, whose smile was already becoming that of a stranger.

"It has been magnificent," she said.

Then I looked around for the old woman, but she had gone out and the last I saw of her was a grey figure beyond the window, hobbling desperately across the station like some maimed and peculiar animal, trying to catch the last métro.

THE

LIVELY

ANATOMY

OF GOD

The Lively Anatomy of God

I WAS born in Trondheim. Do you know it? The whole city stands in the shadow of the church. I used to imagine that it cast its shadow over our house. No, I did not imagine it. Even in summer, at midnight, when the sun was still bright in the sky, we sat outside and its shadow fell over us.

"Brother," said Per. "I feel a draft."

He was very sensitive to drafts. My mother would cover him with her shawl while my father looked on, picking his teeth with an ivory toothpick he brought from India in his sailing days. We would sit in the garden eating minced bread and the cloudberry jam my mother canned all summer. Ever since he came home from the sea, my father has been thinking of his soul, quietly.

"Give us a prayer," he'll say to Per on those nights, because when he looks at the light he thinks of the dark as well. "Or sing to us."

How he can sing! A long clear note, aching, plaintive, as if it came from a great distance, as if somebody working in the fields out of sight was singing to himself. When he sang "The Black Bull of Norroway," you had to wipe your eyes.

On Midsummer's Eve when half the town was dancing in the forest, he sat wrapped in the shawl at the edge of the fire, watching the young men jump over it. What energy! what grace! And I jumped over it and nearly singed my shoes; I jumped because Ragnhild the brewer's daughter was watching. She clapped her hands with the others as I sailed over. And then my brother, hunched like an invalid on the sidelines, began to sing.

> *A thousand years I served for thee,*
> *The glassy hill I clamb for thee,*
> *The bloody shirt I wrang for thee,*
> *And wilt thou not waken and turn to me?*

You can't imagine how it affects people, his singing. Even if I had his voice, I couldn't draw the women as he does; Ragnhild, with her hair falling long and straight over her blue jumper, would not sit timidly at my feet like a deer charmed by the sound. For my brother is dark, with a fine moustache; his very presence seems to imprint the air. Whereas I am blonde, such a towhead that bright sunlight can dissolve me altogether. My eyes are weak, my skin as pale as water, you expect to see fish swimming there and birds flying through me. It's as if I were invisible; people don't notice me out of the sides of their eyes when I come into a room. Whereas my brother can sidle up behind a girl and make her turn around as if a pillar of fire had scorched her.

And he was devout. That made him doubly attractive; everyone knew he was destined for great things. One night —it was just after Easter—he moved all his possessions into the attic. Then he moved up there himself. He was reading *The Paradise of the Holy Father, Being the Histories of Coenobites and Ascetic Fathers of the Deserts of Egypt*. It's a curious book, full of wise sayings: "Eat grass, wear grass, and sleep on grass; then thy heart will become like iron," "Flee from the children of men, and keep silence, and thou shalt live."

My brother began rising at four; he used to wake us all with his praying and his crying out. I had a little ham radio station set up in my room and these devotions used to bother me no end. There was a man in Brazil I talked to regularly, a very old man, nearly blind and gone mad in a skeptical sort of way, but with ears quick like a dog's. He could hear out of the normal frequency and he used to complain about it.

"We're in the rainy season," he'd rasp, "and my ears are a-ringing. Hundreds of insects come out after the rains."

"What does it sound like?" I'd ask.

"Cymbals and bells, cymbals and bells."

Of course static in the reception used to pain him, too; he wanted the best fidelity possible. We spoke to each other in broken German, the only language we had in common. Once when we were conversing about the merits of crop rotation—it was his favorite topic—there came these cries from heaven.

"Oh, lamb of God that takest away the sins of the world!"

"Somebody's cutting in," shouted the old man.

And I explained to him about my brother Per, and how he prayed, and the old man begged me not to tune in when he was praying, as it set up bells in his head.

Along with the praying, my brother took to confessing.

"I confess I thought badly of you, brother," he would say to me. "I thought you stole a five crown piece from my desk."

Or:

"I confess I thought badly of you, Herr Butcher. I have thought you leaned your elbow against the scales when you weighed my mother's roast. I ask your forgiveness."

What can you say when he puts it like that?

"He gets it from his grandfather," says my mother.

Grandfather owned the church in our district when we lived on the farm, before we moved into the shadow of the cathedral. And he too had fits of holiness.

But that wasn't for me, that life. Not me. I wanted to be

79

lots of things: sailor, woodsman, and at last stonecutter. When I was a kid, Eric, Eric the dead, my older brother who worked on the church, used to take me to watch the stonecutters. For that's the queer thing about the church; it has never been finished. They've been working on it now for a thousand years. It burns down every hundred years or so, and then they start all over again. Now they're putting all their efforts on the west facade. They hope to finish it by the millennium.

"Brother," I said to my older brother who was cutting an angel when he fell off the scaffold, "why do you make all these statues where nobody can see them?"

For you can't imagine all there was to look at up there on the windy scaffold; the saints with the faces of local heroes running along the niches and above them, set in rows like teeth, the martyrs with their heads tucked under their arms, the prophets and the judges and angels, all chords hung on some unsung stave of glory. From the ground you could never see the stone flowers, columbine and fleur-de-lis, nor the monkeys rustling the hems of the Virgin Saint Agatha and the Virgin Saint Barbara, who juggled wee castles and lambs like paschal cakes and smuggled crowns under their cloaks. And beyond it all, you could see the churchyard, the coffinmaker's shop with what looked like the smallest of fiddle cases ranged out in front, then the park and the bridge and the small shops, then the houses and farms and the wide fields stretching down to the glittering bay.

"God sees them," said Eric.

And he fell off the scaffolding when he was sixteen. I was only twelve at the time, and Per was ten. He fell off and God saw it, and allowed that his head should be crushed like a pomegranate on the back of a unicorn which would stand on the west tower.

The unicorn was made by another man, an older fellow,

Herr Breman, who had a wife and children away from the church on the other side of the river. He bicycled ten miles to work each morning; in the winter he came on skis.

"I made the beast that killed your brother," he exclaimed in anguish. "Better that it should have killed me."

But everyone told him it was not like that at all. A unicorn killed him, but it could just as well have been a griffin or a peacock. I went with my father to collect my brother's cutting tools.

There they were, chisels and picks, clean as a surgeon's, lying beside my brother's lunchpail on the back of a basilisk which had barely emerged from a stone, under the stonecutter's shed. It was a cornice-piece to go under the angel's feet, the angel whose face my brother was cutting on the west façade when he fell. Herr Breman said he would finish them both; he knew the way of doing it that would have pleased my brother. And he tied up the tools in their leather case and handed them to us, the tears shining on his face.

The coffinmaker, seeing us, had wheeled out his most expensive wares—silver coffins with wheat stalks graven on the lid in gold and fluted shells at the handles, for man is always a pilgrim, said the coffinmaker, *homo viator*, may he rest in peace. All satin-lined for the dead to be comfy. He knew how the fresher the grief the more you imagine that dead bones ache and grow weary, the same as your own.

When they buried my brother on the hill behind the church, I knew I wanted to be a stonecutter, to eat my lunch from a tin pail in the shadow of the church and earn the tools that my brother had carried. I wanted to bring out the wings of the basilisk and the faces of the angels. For the stones were full of such things, he used to say. The stonecarver only frees them, he invents nothing.

Instead of feeling out the face of God, I am a housepainter. During the summer I stand all day on a ladder, painting an antiseptic white on the cottage where Herr Butcher lives with his wife and six bloodhounds. Beyond the eaves I see my brother Per walking down the road, hand in hand with Ragnhild the brewer's daughter whose hair falls long and straight over her blue jumper.

"A little to the left," shouts Herr Butcher, dancing at the foot of the ladder. "You missed a spot."

I get down and move the ladder to the left and run up and paint the spot. Herr Butcher is striding up and down with his six bloodhounds, telling me that man is evil, that he should extinguish himself and leave the earth to the animals as it was on the fifth day before man came. I see my brother Per has put his arm around Ragnhild's shoulder and she leans her head shyly against him.

"A little lower down," shouts Herr Butcher. "You're letting it drip."

When I come home, the family sits in the garden and listens to the hymns blowing from the fields at the edge of town.

"Heavenly God," says my father. "The Methodists are back."

They come every summer, a straggling little band seeking converts. They set up their tent at the edge of town, but even so, it's a bad place for Methodists, for there's no place they can go where the shadow of the church does not fall.

The first year they appeared, my brother Per was fourteen and I was sixteen. We had gone walking in the west pasture beyond the houses to look at the runestone. The runestone is nothing but an outcropping of smooth black rock with crude carvings on it, but the farmer who owns the land has painted the carvings in red, so that you can see very clearly the stickmen and stick-women, the skeletal ships with oars like pocket combs, and the many-legged sun. We stretched ourselves out on the warm stone and puzzled as we always did over the pictures under us.

"Why put a ship in a pasture?" asked Per.

"Because it wasn't always pasture," I said. "It was once the edge of the sea, and there must have been people here who came to worship the sun."

It is one of the few things I remember learning in primary school.

"Like us," said Per. "We're worshipping the sun now, aren't we?"

"Like us," I said.

Per closed his eyes. And then the first hymns stirred the air, like the rumblings of a distant storm. My brother sat up with a start as if he'd felt the breath of God scourging him.

"It's angels," he cried.

Zip-zip-zipppple—the heavenly voices rasped and crackled with static.

"It's not angels," I said. "Let's go and see."

If ever I wanted the power to bring forth the faces of angels, it was then. For my brother desired intensely to see them, to have a sign. Not that he doubted God, only that a sign from heaven would show you were becoming wiser in the ways of the spirit. All the saints had been given signs and some very ordinary folk as well. He was ready to turn the slightest thing into a sign—a strange dog following him, a bird at his window, a stranger asking him for directions.

The hymns led us to a mouse-colored tent with a loud-speaker system stuck on it like a weather vane. We crept inside; someone at the door handed us a leaflet telling us to repent and we sat down on a bench at the back, among a throng of men and women and a few children who listened atten-

83

tively to the speaker. The speaker was, I presumed, the minister, yet he wore no robe, only his suit, and he had loosened his tie so that it hung like a paisley noose around his neck. His cheeks glistened with sweat and his voice grew shrill with effort. He had been speaking for some time, and we arrived for the climax.

"If you have faith and doubt not, which of you shall not move mountains? For whom shall the mountain not cast itself into the sea? Which of you, if he asks for bread, shall receive a stone?"

Then he looked straight at Per and dropped his voice to a whisper, as if these words were meant only for him:

"But they that wait upon the Lord shall renew their strength; they shall mount up with wings as eagles."

It hit him like a sign, the sign he had wanted so long. He did not speak a word all the way home. He went straight up to his room—fortunately he had not yet moved to the attic —and climbed out on the roof and jumped off.

My mother was picking cloudberries in the back yard when he flew past her. She thought at first she had seen a giant bird; she even heard the fluttering of wings. Then the bushes smashed apart under her hand and she saw Per crumpled in the middle of them.

"He's dead!" she cried out, and my father and I came running.

We pulled him to his feet, sputtering and coughing.

"I wanted to fly. Did I fly?" His shirt was torn and berry-stained, and nettles and leaves clung to his hair.

"You wanted to fly!" exclaimed my mother.

"It was for God," he said, barely audible.

My mother shook her head.

"God kept you in His hand. Do you think He wants you to try Him like that?"

They sent for the priest, who warned him against succumbing to the snares of the devil. After all, when the devil invited Christ to cast Himself down from the pinnacle of the temple, didn't He decline the offer, though He had dominions and seraphim at His command?

But there was no danger, our roof is low, I jumped it myself the next day and nobody sent the priest after me. When Per saw that, he tried it again, and soon it was a regular game with us. After supper my mother and father would sip their coffee in the garden and read the paper, while Per and I took turns jumping off the roof.

"Look here, wife, another church burned to the ground, in Røros!"

Thump!

"Wasn't it only last week that a church caught fire somewhere?"

Thump! We would spring up, agile as cats, as if the earth were a trampoline. Per had no illusions about flying now, but it was great fun. And my mother didn't mind, but she said we must keep clear of her cloudberries.

I can't tell you how intolerable it is, living with someone who wishes to make himself a saint. Yet it seemed to me that my brother was beginning to look holy, not like the saints and prophets that people painted in the country churches long ago, when our country was Catholic, for inside the haloes they could only paint what they knew: their own faces. No, he looked more like those tortured Spanish saints you sometimes see in Catholic churches today, with a waxen pallor and dark hair and glittering eyes; a burning, inhuman—or superhuman—presence.

He was the head of our Confirmation class, he was the star pupil in Scriptures and Theology when we were students at the gymnasium together, and in the summer of his twentieth year he was allowed to sing the part of Saint Olaf in the pageant given on the Saint's day. For the man who sings that part must be wise as well as musical, and my brother distinguished himself at Thursday prayers in a way that no one present will ever forget.

Only old women come to Thursday night prayers, and a few young boys brought by their mothers and grandmothers. But my brother always goes. He sits a little apart from my mother, to show he has come of his own volition. I go only rarely. The priest himself leads the service, but first he takes roll to see who among the faithful should be remembered in his private prayers for treasures in heaven, and who among the slothful needs to be prodded for the sake of his soul. He calls your name and you must answer with all the scriptural verses you can think of. It is a fearful and humiliating experience. In the summer, even the most diligent avoid it. But early in July, two weeks or so before Saint Olaf's Eve, everyone comes, there is festival in the air, someone is chosen to play the saint, and no one wants to be left out.

Therefore I was present on the day my brother distinguished himself at Thursday prayers. The priest stands at the head of the aisle and opens his small black book.

"Herr Hanson!"

The butcher stands up.

"And thou shalt offer every day a bullock for a sin offering for atonement," stammers the butcher. Then he sits down. It is the same one he gave last time, several months ago, and the priest waits.

"Nothing more, Herr Hanson? Well, then, Herr Bjørke!"

My father stands up.

"They that go down to the sea in ships, that do business in great waters."

I know he can say whole chapters if he wants to, yet all the words have disappeared, and he sits down sheepishly. Then the priest calls on the wives, and the butcher's wife gives a sentence from the book of Proverbs about the good house-wife, and my mother remembers a bit from the story of Martha and Mary, but none of them can go further than one sentence, and all their speeches end in confusion. For the minister has a fierce eye; one is glass, that is the mild one, the other is real, that is the fierce one. And then he turns his eye upon my brother Per. And Per looks at him without flinching and stands up.

"The vision of Isaiah the son of Amoz, which he saw concerning Judah and Jerusalem in the days of Uzziah, Jotham, Ahaz, and Hezekiah, kings of Judah."

He pauses, the people wait for him to sit down, but he is just getting his breath.

"Hear, O heavens, and give ear, O earth: for the Lord hath spoken . . ."

And then, for fear he will be interrupted, he does not stop for breath but rushes on, his tongue unrolling the book like a scroll, showing the future as it closes upon the past, until the whole tale has flowed over us. It is the priest who sits down now. And everyone knows that my brother has won, that he will be a priest some day and maybe even a bishop, and the stonecutters will put his face on the west facade.

That was when I first moved into the church. It was Saint Olaf's Eve, and from the scaffold on the west facade you could see the pilgrim ships coming into the bay. I didn't intend to stay in the church, you understand, just to disappear for a while, to worry people a bit, so that they might think I had died. Then they will be glad to see me, I thought. My mother will put her shawl around me in the garden, my father will hear from Herr Butcher how well I've painted his house, and my mother will say,

"He gets it from his grandfather."

For my other grandfather was one of the great rose-painters. He painted saints and dwarfs and queer beasts on the doors of churches in Hallingdal and Telemark. Why a rose-painter? Because he had heard that in the great churches of Europe, cherubs and demons encrusted everything, till there was not an inch of space left. But he had never been to the continent, he did not know how the creatures of divine revelation looked, only that they were scrolled and splayed and very beautiful. Where he did not understand, he painted roses. They were the sumptuous flowering of his ignorance.

They will speak of him, I thought, when I saw myself sitting with my mother's shawl on my shoulders. I know now that no one wants the dead to return.

I brought with me a loaf of bread, two sausages, a round of cheese, a jar of cloudberry jam, and my radio equipment. The reception from the top of the cathedral is excellent. I had a long room to myself over the side aisle, where I could run up and down like a squirrel, between the Gallery of the Prophets and the buttresses that curved into the wall and seemed to crowd it with wheels, suggesting the outer shore of a gigantic clock.

There was a niche in the boards at one end of the floor, and if you lay on your stomach you could see the crowds, coming from the bright sunlight into the cool darkness of the church. It was already early evening by the time I had my radio rigged up. Below me and around me, the sun turned the windows to wine and honey.

"You sound as if you're speaking in a wind," said the man from Brazil.

"It's the Eve of Saint Olaf," I told him, "and I'm lying on

the ceiling of the church, watching the people through a hole the size of my thumb."

High over the choir, the organ began to pump its heavy blurred chords and shrill scales, so that the floor buzzed under my stomach, and my breastbone thwanged like a Jew's harp.

"What's happening now?"

"The people are coming in."

"Yes, yes, I hear that. But what are they doing?"

"They're taking their seats."

"Is it folding chairs I hear?"

"There are some folding chairs, on account of the crowds, for those who have come too late to find room in the pews."

Now a hush dropped over everyone. And through the niche in the floor I saw my brother, swaying like a lily in his white robe, step in front of the altar. The organ piped one long note, such as you'd expect from a shepherd playing his flute in the evening out of sight. Then my brother opened his mouth and began to sing.

It leaped to the rafters, it flooded the crypt with light, it beat on the tombs of the dead kings and the ears of the pilgrims who overflowed the nave into the side aisles. The loudspeaker carried it to those outside; it's filling the city now, I thought, the city is filling up with music.

> *Where is God my maker*
> *Who giveth songs in the night?*

And no one doubted but that this was Saint Olaf himself, calling on the Lord to slay the dragons that slink out of the dark lands far to the north, or waking one morning to find the towers of heaven spinning themselves in the air over his head.

When the last note passed out of hearing, the minister rushed to fill the vacuum with a stout prayer, for too much music leads the soul into unholy desires, away from the narrow path of duty. The organ was subdued to a faint quiver of chords.

Put on the whole armor of God, that ye may be able to stand against the wiles of the devil. Take the shield of faith, wherewith ye shall be able to quench the fiery darts of the wicked.

And as he was saying these things, his voice slipped out behind another voice, which stepped into its place and boomed through the sanctuary.

"Splendid singing. I like that. More singing! That's what we need—"

—helmet of salvation, and the sword of the Spirit, which is—

"Now a good song I can stand. But those prayers—cymbals and bells, cymbals and bells."

The organ stopped abruptly. A kind of fluttering seized the congregation, and hundreds of voices began to whirr.

"I hear the murmur of bees," said the man from Brazil, and the rafters shook with it: *murmur of bees!*

And from out of the silence that had fallen on everything below me, an anonymous cry rose up.

"God has spoken!"

Then I thought I had better come down at once, for they might search the church. Better to have them think it was God than a voice from Brazil caught on the minister's frequency. I took my bundle of food and my radio and left quietly, and an hour later I walked into the kitchen where my mother was making herring cakes.

"We missed you at services," she said, hardly glancing up at me. "I suppose you heard. Who can explain it? Your brother sang, he sang so beautifully. Then the minister prayed and God himself interrupted. 'Splendid singing! I like that. More singing!' A thousand people heard it."

Well, I knew things would be worse than ever at home

after that. I fell back on my old trade. I painted the widow Ingstad's house on our street and two barns at the edge of town—that took me a while, I can tell you, what with the white trim and all the carving at the top. And then there were the animals rooting and snorting below me, morning and evening, and in between times they stood around in the field watching my every move and waiting for me to miss a spot.

Per was asked by those who had heard him sing to pray over sick relatives and stillborn calves. He said enormous prayers at breakfast and dinner that blessed the food to our use and left it cold and uneatable. He wore black at home and my mother doted on him.

Then I got a commission to repaint the church at Røros, which the parish had rebuilt after the fire, and this took me out of the house for a week. My first night home, sirens woke us up, and the next morning at market everyone was talking about it:

"Someone has burned down the church on the Halvsted farm. To the ground."

"It was the Methodists," said my father, and he believed it.

But the Methodists were gone, and like swallows they would not return for another season. And then, before this news was cold, another church blazed up in a small town to the north, a wooden church with a fine dragon carved on the roof.

"No one can replace such things anymore," said Herr Butcher as he leaned on the scales and weighed my mother's roast. "Who among us knows what a dragon looks like, except the stonecutters?"

One day my brother was accepted at the divinity school with honors and Ragnhild, with her straight hair falling down her blue jumper, consented to wait for him. She would marry no one else, and while she was waiting she would sew her linens as her mother had done, and when he came home she would hang them out on the line so that the neighbors would see what a fine wife he was getting. And the holier he became, the more she loved him. Women like to feel they are serving something beyond themselves, and what could be more noble than a servant of God and one for whom God has spoken?

So I decided to move again to the church. I had not stayed there long enough. I tied some of my clothes in a bundle and took them down to the bay and left them on the shore, at the high tideline, among the pebbles and broken shells.

It was August now and very hot, it was unusually hot for Norway. The room over the aisle was stifling. At night it did not cool off but kept all the heat inside, like a giant kiln. I decided to sleep downstairs in the sanctuary.

The first night I slept on the pews and when I woke, I thought I must have rolled off and broken my back. The second night I was luckier. From the west tower I watched the coffin-maker, whose shop stood conveniently between the church and the cemetery, rolling his wares about. Business was good, there must have been a fishing accident off the coast, I thought, as he danced about before the successions of widows and orphans. He lined the coffins up in the yard to show how the sunlight glowed on the graven garlands of wheat and the silver shells on the handles—for man is always a pilgrim in this life, he would be saying to them now: *homo viator, may he rest in peace.*

He closed shop at five and left a fine bronze coffin on castors in his yard. A pity the dew should rust it, I thought; better to bring it into the sanctuary for safekeeping. The streets were empty, everyone had gone home for dinner. I darted out and wheeled it across the lawn through the side door and parked it to the left of the altar, near the sacristy and the stairs. Under the lid, it was quilted with white satin, and several hours later I lay down inside and went to sleep.

I woke up before morning to a crackling noise, as if someone had crunched my sleep into a ball. Startled, I sat up. There was a strong smell of gasoline.

Someone was lighting the altar.

Two places were burning, he was lighting a third over my head. I leaped up in terror. The man let out a cry, the can he was carrying clattered to the ground, and he ran down the aisle. At the doorway I wrestled him to the ground but found I was grappling with a dead man; he had already fainted away. So I carried him to the back of the church where the bells of the east tower let down their ropes, and having no knife, I tied him with the ropes as they hung.

And that was how they found him, a stranger ringing the town awake with the weight of his body in the middle of the night, like a man left on the gallows.

In the newspaper which the verger leaves in the church parlors, I read of the miracle, of how God leaped from the darkness and spared a man already condemned to die. He had escaped from a prison in Sweden and lived in the mountains for several months, plotting his revenge on the human race and the order of things which held them together. He had gone in to burn the church and met his angel and repented so completely that he wanted to take vows and live the life of a monk on some secluded island. For God had shown Himself as a sign, His face had blazed like the sun in the darkness.

On the back page I noticed a small item: *Housepainter Drowns Self.*

So if that's how things stand, I told myself, it's better to live in the church. There are others who can paint houses, there is no one to do the work that I do. Can I help it if in the darkness they think I am God? I sing to myself, for I did not bring my radio here, and the deacon thinks he is hearing angels. I am seen moving behind the altar, and the verger swears he has seen the living God.

And something has happened to my own sight of late. It was never very good, I have the weak eyes of an albino. Is it looking off into the distance for so many hours that has made them so far-sighted? I can hardly read the papers anymore and I have no glasses. Only the workmen come close to me now, when I am sitting in the west tower, and they do not know how close their faces are to mine. They still bring schoolchildren up on the scaffold to see the angels, and the children still ask,

"When will you be finished?"

"Never."

"And who will see all this when the scaffolding comes down?"

"God will see it."

But one morning I heard my brother's voice; it was Per come home from divinity school in the spring. He had climbed up the scaffolding early in the morning to be alone and to pray.

"God, give me a sign—I am utterly forsaken."

He's showing off his rhetoric as usual, I thought. Who would forsake Per, the chosen servant of the Lord?

"If I had married her, then she would not have left me!" he cried out bitterly. "I gave up everything for You."

Then I thought he was going to throw himself off the scaffold onto the stones below. I was in a panic. From where I sat, I could see the back of his head, I could see him teetering.

"A sign, Lord, only a sign!"

Desperately, in my crazy cracked voice, I began to sing,

> *A thousand years I served for thee,*
> *The glassy hill I clamb for thee,*
> *The bloody shirt I wrang for thee,*
> *And wilt thou not waken and turn to me?*

Then I thought he would fall off from amazement. He lay flat on his stomach on the scaffold with his arms dangling down over the sides.

"Pardon, my Lord," he whispered.

And now such stories circulate about me as you can't imagine, let alone believe. I hear the stonecutters tell them to each other, how I healed a man here, helped a man there. It was not what I set out to do. And my brother is the priest now, he was chosen when the old one died. The old one lies in the churchyard near my brother Eric. With a single glance I can join the living and the dead, the old sailor living and his young son dead, the old priest fallen in the service of God and his successor.

It was not what I set out to do. I would rather be down below, cutting angels to praise the Lord than to be the hidden scaffolding of faith.

"Pardon, my Lord!"

And in that moment when the Creator of the universe, Who holds all in His gaze, Who commands the morning and fathers the rain, Who has measured the waters in the hollow of His hand and comprehended the dust of the earth in a measure and weighed the mountains in scales and the hills in a balance, when He turns His mighty Presence on one man to forgive him, how those He chooses quake for joy! As if they had slept all their lives in a stone, they waken, they rise up, they are born again.

Designed by Edith McKeon

Printed at The Stinehour Press

Bound by Russell-Rutter